E

Nell Nugget
and the COW CAPER

SIMON & SCHUSTER
BOOKS FOR YOUNG READERS

SIMON & SCHUSTER BOOKS FOR YOUNG READERS
An imprint of Simon & Schuster Children's Publishing Division
1230 Avenue of the Americas, New York, New York 10020
Text copyright © 1996 by Judith Ross Enderle and Stephanie Gordon Tessler
Illustrations copyright © 1996 by Paul Yalowitz
All rights reserved including the right of reproduction in whole or in part in any form.
SIMON & SCHUSTER BOOKS FOR YOUNG READERS is a trademark of Simon & Schuster.
Designed by Lucille Chomowicz and Heather Wood
The text of this book is set in Bramley Light.
The illustrations in this book were first drawn with ebony pencil on bristol plate paper and then
colored over with Derwent color pencils. Because the artist is right-handed, he starts drawing on
the left side of the paper and moves to the right so that the picture won't smudge. The paper is
very smooth, and only the artist knows where that mysterious texture comes from.
The illustrations were color-separated and reproduced using four-color process.
Manufactured in the United States of America • First Edition 10 9 8 7 6 5 4 3 2 1

Library of Congress Cataloging-in-Publication Data
Enderle, Judith Ross.
Nell Nugget and the cow caper / story by Judith Ross Enderle & Stephanie Gordon Tessler
pictures by Paul Yalowitz — 1st ed.
p.   cm.
Summary: When her best cow, Goldie, is stolen by the robber Nasty Galoot, Nell Nugget uses
her horse, her dog, her piano, and her other forty-eight cows to get Goldie back. ISBN 0-689-80502-0
[1. West (U.S.)—Fiction. 2. Robbers and outlaws—Fiction.]   I. Tessler, Stephanie Gordon.
II. Yalowitz, Paul, ill.   III. Title.   PZ7.E6966Ne   1996   [E]—dc20   94-10189   CIP   AC

YIPPEE-YI-YAY!

YIPPEE-YI-YO!

Way out West, on the Bar None Ranch, Nell Nugget lived with her horse, Pay Dirt, and her little dog, Dust.

One morning out on the range, Nell counted her cows. "One, two, three," Nell began. "Forty-six, forty-seven, forty-eight," she ended.

"But there should be forty-nine. Where is Goldie? My best cow is missing!" Nell cried.

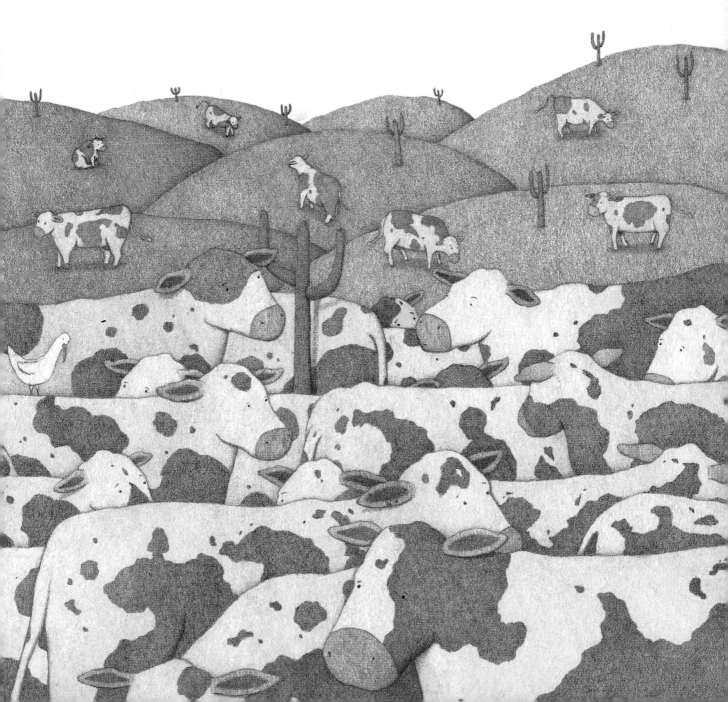

GOLDIE!

Nell looked high
till noon.

GOLDIE?

Nell looked low
till sunset.

"Goldie!" she called and called. But there was no trace of her best cow.

So CLIP CLOPPITY CLIP

Nell and Pay Dirt rode back to the ranch.

And her little dog, Dust, trailed behind.

That night Nell played her piano. PLINK, PLUNKETY, PLINK. "Where, oh where, has my Goldie gone?" Nell sang. "Where, oh where, can she be?" she crooned. PLINK, PLUNKETY, PLINK.

Campfire songs carried out the windows. Campfire songs carried uphill and down. Campfire songs carried out to the open range.

Nell sang and sang until her cows came home—all but Goldie.

PLINK

PLUNKETY

PLINK

PLINK
PLUNKETY
PLINK

PLUNKETY

The next morning Nell called on Sheriff Doolittle. "Goldie is gone!" Nell cried. "Please help me find my best cow."

"I'd surely like to help, little gal," said the sheriff, "but I'm hot on the trail of Nasty Galoot, the worst rustlin' robber in the West, the baddest bad man anywhere."

CLOPP**I**TY

CLIP CLIP

"My stars!" Nell said. "Then I'll have to find Goldie myself."
So CLIP, CLOPPITY, CLIP, Nell rode off on her horse,
Pay Dirt.
  And her little dog, Dust, trailed behind.

Nell looked high and low. Nell looked near and far.

And then—"Pay Dirt!" she cried. "Big horse prints in the tumbleweeds; Goldie's little cow prints in the cactus!"

The trail led uphill. The trail led downhill.

"Whoa, Pay Dirt," said Nell. "Do you hear what I hear?"

"MOO, MOO, MOO-O-O-O!"

"Oh dear, Dust. That's Goldie's 'Help me!' moo!" said Nell.

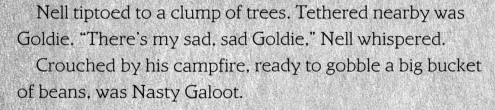

Nell tiptoed to a clump of trees. Tethered nearby was
Goldie. "There's my sad, sad Goldie," Nell whispered.
    Crouched by his campfire, ready to gobble a big bucket
of beans, was Nasty Galoot.
    "And there's the baddest bad man who stole her," said Nell.

Nell stood tall in her five-gallon hat. She marched right up to that cow rustler. "I am Nell Nugget," she said. "Goldie is my cow."

"I am Nasty Galoot," he said. "Goldie is my cow now."

"She is not," said Nell. "Please give her back."

"No," said Nasty.

"You are the baddest bad man anywhere," said Nell.

"Ha, ha, ha," said Nasty Galoot. Then WAHOO! he tossed his beans into the air.

PLOP, PLOPPITY, PLOP, beans fell everywhere.

Ducking and dodging, slipping and sliding, Nell ran for Goldie.

But Nasty got there first. He grabbed Goldie's rope, leaped on his horse, and away he rode.

"MOO, MOO, MOO-O-O-O!" Goldie cried.

"BOO, HOO, HOO-O-O-O!" Nell cried.

Nell's cowgirl blood was boiling. "This is no time for tears," Nell told herself. "That no-good Nasty won't get away with my best cow," she said. "Time to get a move on, Pay Dirt," she called.

And her little dog, Dust, trailed behind.

Nell caught up to Nasty at Muddy Mud Creek, the slickiest, stickiest water in the West.

Brave Dust raced ahead into the camp. "WOOF, WOOF, WOOF," he barked.

"Ha, ha, ha, you rustlin' robber, you baddest bad man," Nell cried. "Now give me back my cow."

WOOF
WOOF
WOOF

Nasty Galoot sneered. "Ho, ho, ho," he laughed.
"I am not afraid of your little doggy."
He threw his lasso around Dust.

"WOO, WOO, WOO-O-O-O," Dust howled.
"MOO, MOO, MOO-O-O-O," Goldie cried.

Ho, ho, ho

WOO   WOO

CLIP

CLOPPITY

CLIP

MOO   MOO-O-O-O

O-O-O

"Now I have your cow and your dog, Nell Nugget," said
Nasty Galoot.

"We'll see about that!" said Nell.

"Don't cry, Goldie," she called. "Be brave, Dust," she said.
"I'll be back."

So CLIP, CLOPPITY, CLIP, Nell rode away as fast as the wind.

Back at the ranch, Nell lassoed her piano. "Time to get a move on," she said.

Nell and Pay Dirt raced uphill and down. They raced past the trees and the rocks. They raced back to Nasty Galoot's camp.

Nell watched and waited until BREEP, BREEP, BREEP, the frogs in the mud sang—until CRICK, CRICK, CRICK, the crickets by the creek clicked—until, round as an orange, the full moon rose.

Soon Nasty Galoot hung his britches on a tree branch; then he slid into his bedroll.

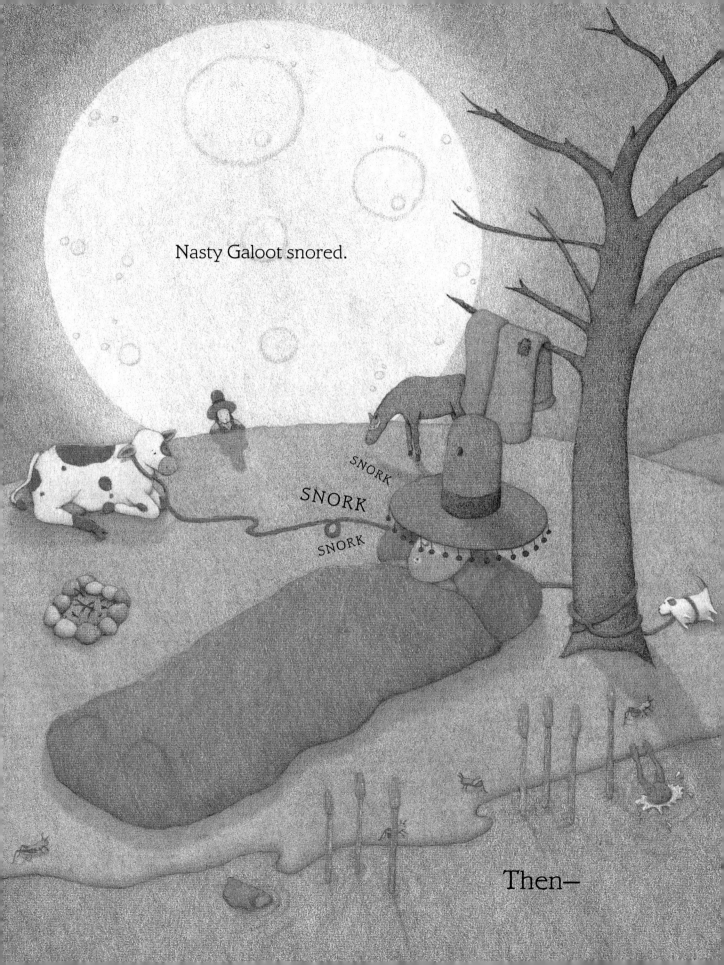

Nasty Galoot snored.

SNORK

SNORK

SNORK

Then—

PLINK, PLUNKETY, PLINK. Nell played her piano.
"Where, oh where, have my little cows gone?" she sang.
"Where, oh where, can they be?" Nell crooned.

Campfire songs carried past the creek and trees.
Campfire songs carried uphill and down. Campfire songs
carried out to the open range.

PLUNKETY

PLINK

PLINK

PLINK
PLUNKETY
PLINK

Nasty Galoot slept on.

SNORK

SNORK

SNORK

PLINK

Until—

GALUMP GALUMP GALUMP

Cows came from the east.

GALUMP GALUMP

Cows came from the west.

Cows stepped on Nasty's nose.
Cows stepped on Nasty's toes.
   Forty-eight cows came to hear
campfire songs.

"Ouch! Ooh!" shouted Nasty. He bounded out of his bedroll. He scrambled across the cows. He shinnied up the nearest tree.

"MOO, MOO, MOO. MOO, MOO, MOO." Goldie and forty-eight cows sang campfire songs with Nell.

"Stop that singing," shouted the baddest bad man anywhere.

"Sure thing, Nasty," said Nell, "but I'm taking my cow. And I'm taking my dog."

She lassoed her piano. "Time to get a move on, Pay Dirt," she said.

MOO

MOO

MOO MOO

MOO

MOO

MOO

MOO

MOO

"Stop!" shouted Nasty.

MOO

MOO

MOO MOO MOO

MOO

MOO MOO

MOO

MOO MOO MOO

Nasty kept climbing, and
he leaped onto a limb.

He bounced once.
He bounced twice.

WAHOO! He landed on Goldie's back.

"Now giddy-up, cow," he yelled.

GALUMP! Goldie walked.
GALUMP! GALUMP! Goldie trotted.

Oh, no!

MOO

GALUMP! GALUMP! GALUMP! Goldie ran—
right to the bank of Muddy Mud Creek.
"Oh, no! Whoa, cow!" shouted Nasty.
Goldie slid to a stop. She lowered her
head. She kicked her back legs.

"Help!" Nasty yelped. "I'm stuck in the mud of Muddy Mud Creek!"

"Sheriff Doolittle will help," Nell said. "I hear he's hot on your trail.

KER-PLOP!

"Time to get a move on, Pay Dirt," Nell called.

Then CLIP CLOPPITY CLIP

Nell and forty-eight cows headed for home. And her best cow, Goldie, made forty-nine.
YIPPEE-YI-YO! YIPPEE-YI-YAY!
And her little dog, Dust, trailed behind.